Who's Who at the Zoo?

By Ellen Weiss
Illustrated by Tom Cooke

Featuring Jim Henson's Sesame Street Muppets

A SESAME STREET/GOLDEN PRESS BOOK
Published by Western Publishing Company, Inc.,
in conjunction with Children's Television Workshop.

It was a beautiful sunny day, and Big Bird, Ernie, and Bert went to the zoo.

"I can't wait to see the ostrich!" said Big Bird. "He's a big bird, too."

"I want to visit the pandas," said Ernie.

"Look, there are some pigeons," said Bert. "Oh, happy day."

"Mr. Snuffle-upagus asked me to say hello to his friend at the zoo," said Big Bird. He took a bag out of his backpack. "He asked me to give his friend these peanuts."

"Who is Snuffy's friend?" asked Ernie.

"Oh, dear!" said Big Bird. "I can't remember."

"Do you mean," said Bert, "that we're supposed to go see somebody, but we don't know who it is? How are we ever going to find Snuffy's friend?"

"Well, I do remember one thing Snuffy told me," said Big Bird. "His friend has four legs."

"That animal has four legs," said Ernie.
"That's a leopard," said Bert.
"Oh, hi, Mr. Leopard," said Big Bird.
"But this is not Snuffy's friend," Big Bird said to Ernie and Bert. "Snuffy's friend doesn't have spots."

"Well, then, maybe it's that rhinoceros," said Ernie. "She has four legs, and she doesn't have any spots."

"No, I don't think so," said Big Bird. "I'm sure Snuffy would have told me if his friend had a great big horn like that."

"Look at those lions!" said Ernie. "Lions have four legs and no horns. One of them must be Snuffy's friend."

"I don't think so," said Big Bird. "Snuffy didn't say anything about a mane."

"These lions have manes on their necks, all right," said Bert.

"Here are the pandas," said Bert. "Maybe that one is Snuffy's friend. He doesn't have a mane."

"I don't know," said Big Bird. "Look at those claws. I'm sure Snuffy's friend doesn't have claws."

"This chimpanzee doesn't have claws," said Ernie.
"That's true, but he has hands," said Big Bird.
"Snuffy would have told me if his friend had real hands!"

"Oh, there's the zebra. Maybe she's Mr. Snuffle-upagus' friend," said Ernie.

Big Bird thought about it. "No, I'm sure Snuffy would have said something about the zebra's black and white stripes. I don't think the zebra is Snuffy's friend."

"What about the giraffe?" asked Ernie. "Maybe he's Snuffy's friend."

"I think Snuffy would have mentioned it if his friend had such a long neck," said Big Bird.

"Oh, look, here's the ostrich!" said Big Bird. "Hello, Mr. Ostrich."

"I'm sure you're not Snuffy's friend," said Bert. "You only have two legs."

"And feathers!" said Ernie. "Hee, hee!"

"Wait a second," said Bert. "All you've told us about Snuffy's friend is that he has four legs. What else do you know about him, Big Bird?"

"Well, let's see. Snuffy said his friend had wrinkly skin," said Big Bird.

"Maybe he's a giant tortoise like that one over there," said Ernie. "I'll bet he even has wrinkles under his shell."

"I don't think it's a tortoise," said Big Bird. "I just remembered that Snuffy's friend has big ears."

"Big ears?" said Bert thoughtfully. "Maybe it's a rabbit!"

"No, it can't be a rabbit," said Big Bird. "Snuffy's friend is very big."

"I know! The hippopotamus!" cried Ernie. "He has four legs, wrinkly skin, and he certainly is big!"

"But," said Big Bird, "the hippopotamus does not have a snuffle."

"A snuffle!?" cried Bert. "You didn't say anything about a snuffle! We'll never find an animal in the zoo with a snuffle!"

"Look! Mr. Elephant has a great big snuffle!" yelled Big Bird.

"That's a trunk," said Bert.

"It looks just like a snuffle to me," said Big Bird. "And he has four legs, wrinkly skin, huge ears, and he's very big."

"Yes, but does he like peanuts?" asked Ernie.

"Let's see," said Big Bird. "Hi, Mr. Elephant. Your friend Mr. Snuffle-upagus sent you these peanuts, and he says hello."

The elephant grabbed the bag with his snuffle-trunk and dumped the peanuts into his mouth.

"The elephant is Snuffy's friend, all right," said Ernie. "He likes the peanuts."

ABCDEFGHI